Big Sister, Little Sister

story and pictures by **Marci Curtis**

DIAL BOOKS FOR YOUNG READERS  **NEW YORK**

To:

From:

Big Sister, Little Sister

story and pictures by **Marci Curtis**

DIAL BOOKS FOR YOUNG READERS NEW YORK

Rodney Curtis

To Skye and Taylor—best sisters, best daughters, best friends.

Thousands of thanks to Nzingha, Sandile, Catherine, Elizabeth, Tiler, Makala, and their families for sharing their sisterly love.

Published by Dial Books for Young Readers
A division of Penguin Putnam Inc.
345 Hudson Street
New York, New York 10014
Copyright © 2000 by Marci Curtis
All rights reserved
Designed by Kimi Weart
Manufactured in China on acid-free paper

Library of Congress Cataloging in Publication Data
Curtis, Marci.
Big sister, little sister/story and pictures by Marci Curtis.—1st ed.
p.   cm.
Summary: Photo illustrations of real-life sisters
accompanied by a rhyming description of sisterhood.
ISBN 0-8037-2482-9 (hardcover)
[1. Sisters—Fiction. 2. Stories in rhyme.] I. Title.
PZ8.3.C93445Bi   2000
[E]—dc21   99-24796   CIP
Special Markets ISBN 978-0-8037-3958-1 Not For Resale
1 3 5 7 9 10 8 6 4 2

This Imagination Library edition is published by Penguin Group (USA), a Pearson company, exclusively for Dolly Parton's Imagination Library, a not-for-profit program designed to inspire a love of reading and learning, sponsored in part by The Dollywood Foundation. Penguin's trade editions of this work are available wherever books are sold.

Big Sister, Little Sister, a love that is so strong.
Big Sister, Little Sister, best friends all year long.

Big Sister and I, *racing* hand in hand.

Little Sister picks the **biggest** pumpkin in the land.

Big Sister shows me how to *yell* **and** Cheer!

"Little Sister, it's okay. I will dry your tear."

Big Sister swipes a bite. "Don't be such a pig !"

"Little Sister, please let go and I'll buy you a *wig*."

Big Sister shows me how to brush my smile.

Little Sister gives the dog a super- *silly* **style.**

Big Sister teaches me to  **.**

Little Sister follows where I *lead* 👣👣👣.

Big Sister takes a sip from my gigantic drink.

"Little Sister, eat some sn❄w. It's very clean . . . I think."

Big Sister and I, **ZIPPED UP** two-in-one.

Little Sister learns how *homework* **is done.**

Big Sister shares her ♪musical♫ gift.

"Little Sister, you can reach—with a little lift."

Big Sister teaches me the sign for "I l♥ve y♥u."

"Little Sister, heels are tricky, especially when you're two."

Big Sister *soars* **with me on a rainy day.**

Little Sister wants to know, "*Now* who's going to play?"

Big Sister's TANTRUMS always make me cry.

Little Sister cracks up—and so do I!

Big Sister helps me draw a chalky **fantasy.**

Little Sister makes a sandy angel out of me.

Big Sister plays a game of hide-and-seek.

Little Sister's bubble 'do is oh so very chic.

Big Sister loves to comb and braid my hair.

Little Sister skips with me. We make a springy pair!

**Big Sister, Little Sister, best forever friends.
Big and Little Sister, a love that never ends.**

Big brother, little **brother, our adventures never end.**
We'll always have each other and you'll always be my friend.

I have 5 and you have 1—isn't that a shame?

Little brother **looks** like me, but we are **NOT** the same.

Though we're not blood brothers, we are brothers of the heart.

Big brother and I, adopted from the **start**.

Big brother has the fastest peel in the West.

Go ahead. Don't be scared. It's just a butterfly.

Big brother's there for me when I start to cry.

Little brother drools, but I've got super-spit.

Tug his **tail** little brother—and maybe he'll pull us?

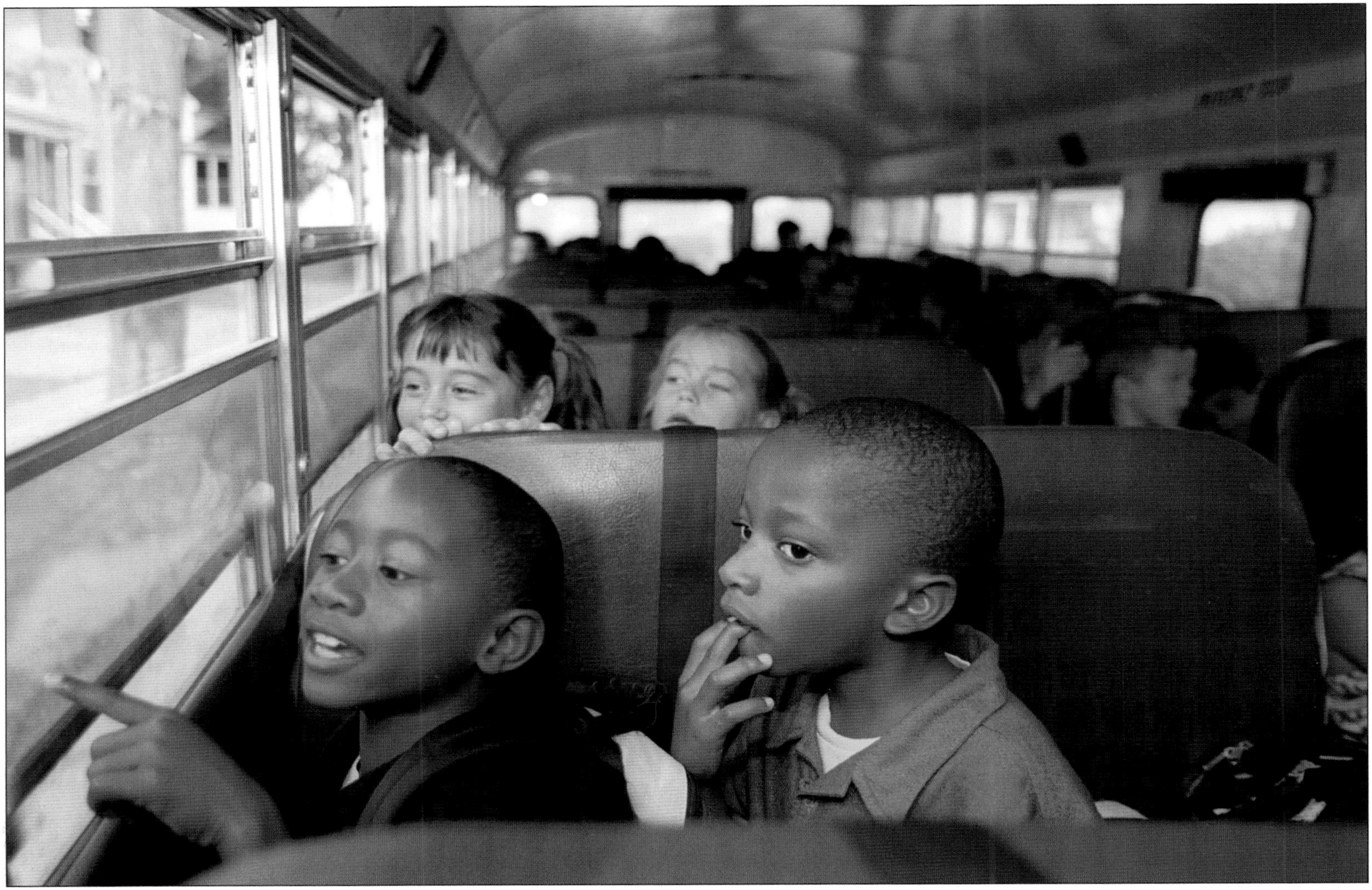

Big brother sits with me my first time on the .

We're munching hanging **donuts** dangling in the air.

Little brother, don't you DARE! Hands off my underwear!

Let's bring Mom the pretty part of her favorite flowers.

Little brother's working hard to fix my SUPER powers.

Watch out!, brother! You'll get more than a peck!

Big brother and I race home *neck* and *neck*.

Kiss my *fish*, make a wish, then I'll set him free.

Little brother's got huge MUSCLES just like me!

I'm going to get you nice and *muddy*.

Big brother is my *topsy-turvy* buddy.

Make two loops, yank 'em tight! Yup, that knot looks right.

Big brother creams me in a pillow ✦fight!✦

Get off, little brother, before our pumpkin squishes.

Big brother blowing bubbles while we do the dishes.

Aim your foot, add some power — now you're really KiCkin'!

Little brother, open wide! **WORMS** taste just like chicken.

Big brother, little brother, buddies true and strong.

Life is truly **twice** as *fun* since he came along.

For Rodney—best hubby, best friend, best soul mate 'til the end.

Big thanks to the big and little brothers:

Sam and **N**ate, **A**lejandro and **A**ntonio, **J**esse and **M**iles,
Zack and **A**li, and my nephews **C**aleb and **A**sher—
it was a pleasure watching you all grow up!

And thanks, too, to the parents and siblings of these wonderful boys
and to the big and little sisters hiding in the book.

Published by Dial Books for Young Readers • A division of Penguin Young Readers Group
345 Hudson Street • New York, New York 10014
Copyright © 2004 by Marci Curtis • All rights reserved • Text set in Triplex
Manufactured in China on acid-free paper
Library of Congress Cataloging-in-Publication Data • Curtis, Marci.
Big brother, little brother / story and pictures by Marci Curtis. • p.   cm.
Summary: Photographs and rhyming text show both the fun and trials of having a big or little brother.
ISBN 0-8037-2870-0 • [1. Brothers—Fiction. 2. Stories in rhyme.] I. Title. PZ8.3.C93445Bg 2004 [E]—dc21   2003009102
Special Markets ISBN 978-0-8037-3958-1 Not For Resale
1 3 5 7 9 10 8 6 4 2

This Imagination Library edition is published by Penguin Group (USA), a Pearson company, exclusively for Dolly Parton's Imagination Library, a not-for-profit program designed to inspire a love of reading and learning, sponsored in part by The Dollywood Foundation. Penguin's trade editions of this work are available wherever books are sold.

DIAL BOOKS FOR YOUNG READERS  NEW YORK

BIG BROTHER, LITTLE BROTHER

Story and pictures by **MARCI CURTIS**

BIG BROTHER, LITTLE BROTHER

Story and pictures by **MARCI CURTIS**

DIAL BOOKS FOR YOUNG READERS · NEW YORK